Contents

'Wakey! Wakey!'

'Lovely Porridge!'

'Wabbit! Wabbit!'

'Ssssh!'

'Ready?'

Reading Ladder

'Wakey-wakey!'

When the alarm went off, Nicky and Tasha sat up in their beds and stared. Mum wasn't there, but the cassette-player was on the floor by Little Joe's cot.

In front of it was a note.

'Press Play,' said the note.

That was all.

'Go on, then,' said Tasha. 'Press Play.'

So Nicky slid out of bed and pressed Play.
They both watched as the tape inside started
to go round and round, and out came their
mother's cheerful early
morning voice.

'Wakey-wakey!'

'Creepy!' said Nicky, and Little Joe gripped his cot bars and pushed out his bottom lip, ready to cry, as the voice went on.

'I had to go in to work really early today. And your dad had to work all night, so he's still sleeping.'

'We'll have to sort ourselves out, then,' muttered Tasha.

'*You'll have to sort yourselves out,*' Mum's voice echoed through the room.

Huh!

Little Joe burst into tears. They spurted out so hard they missed his face completely, and fell on the carpet.

'*You'd better do Little Joe first*,' their mother's voice floated out. '*He might be a bit upset, hearing my voice, but me not being there.*'

'Too right,' said Nicky, and he went across to haul Little Joe over the bars of the cot.

As soon as he felt safe in his brother's arms, Little Joe stopped crying and started to poke his fingers in Nicky's ears. Nicky dumped him down on the potty.

'I'll dress him,' he said to Tasha, 'if you'll feed him.'

'No, no, no, no, no, no,' said Tasha. 'He spat porridge all down me yesterday. I'll dress him. You feed him.'

'We'll toss for it,' said Nicky.

He was just breaking into Tasha's money box for a coin when their mother's voice started up again.

'Nicky, you change him. And, Tasha, you feed him.'

'Thanks, Mum,' groaned Tasha. 'Thanks a bunch!'

'*Now,*' said the voice. '*While Nicky's sorting out Little Joe, Tasha can get dressed, and carry me down carefully into the kitchen.*'

'What?' Tasha said. 'What is she on about?'

Nicky took Little Joe's hand and tugged him over to a pile of fresh clothes beside the cot.

'She means the cassette-player,' said Nicky. 'She means you have to carry it downstairs.'

'Why?'

'I don't know,' Nicky said. 'So she can keep bossing us about, I suppose.'

'Hmph!' said Tasha, who was always a little bit grumpy in the mornings.

Draping her clean clothes over the cassette-player, she picked it up and carried it, very carefully, as far as the top of the stairs.

Then she put it down safely and went into the bathroom with her clothes.

She was just drying her face when, outside the door, she heard a strange whispering.

'What is it?' she called.

Nobody answered, but the whispering carried on.

'Is that you, Nicky?' Tasha shouted. 'What do you want?'

Eh?

He didn't answer, but the whispering kept up.

'Say it louder!' yelled Tasha. 'I can't hear you!'

She stopped to listen. The whispering was still going on outside the door.

'Speak up!' bellowed Tasha. 'Speak up! Speak up! Speak up!'

She flung the door open, and rushed out.
The tape was still going. And so was her
mother's voice, in a whisper.

'. . . so remember what I say, you're not to
wake Daddy up unless you really need him, so
that means you've got to keep very, very quiet all
the time you're in the bathroom . . .'

'Oh, gggrrrr!' growled Tasha.

But she growled it quietly.

'Lovely Porridge!'

Tasha! Tasha!

Little Joe sat in the highchair and banged his fist on the tray.

'Don't forget to strap him in properly,' Tasha said, guessing the next bit on the tape.

'*Don't forget to strap Joe in properly,*' came from the tape. '*I've made his porridge. All you have to do is heat it up.*'

Stirring the porridge, Tasha opened and closed her mouth like an actor on telly with the sound turned down while her mother's voice poured off the tape.

16

'I hope you've chosen something sensible to
wear, Tasha. It looks pretty chilly out there. I
hope you're not wearing something silly like that
thin cotton cowboy shirt.'

Tasha looked down at her thin cotton
cowboy shirt.

'You should be wearing something nice and
warm, like that pretty red woolly Granny knitted
for you.'

Tasha leaned over the pan full of Little Joe's porridge and pretended to throw up in it.

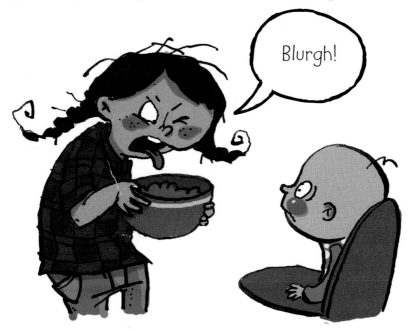

Little Joe's eyes widened. Then he stuck out his bottom lip, ready to cry again.

'It's all right,' Tasha told him. 'I didn't do anything. I was only joking. Here it comes now. Lovely porridge!'

She put the bowl on his tray, and handed him the spoon.

'Don't want it!' said
Little Joe.

'Course you do,' said Tasha.
'Don't!'
'Do!'

'He doesn't want it
because he thinks you threw
up in it,' said Nicky.

Tasha turned to Little Joe. 'Look,' she said
to him. 'Watch.'

Leaning over the bowl, she pretended to
throw up in it all over again.

'See?' she told him. 'Jokey-jokey! There's
nothing wrong with the porridge.'

Little Joe banged his spoon on the tray.

'Jokey-jokey!' he shouted. 'Jokey-jokey!'

'He wants you to do it again,' said Nicky.

'Well, he's out of luck,' said Tasha.

Just at that moment, out of the cassette-player, their mother's voice floated across the room. '*I hope you're making sure Little Joe's eating his breakfast.*'

Sighing, Tasha did it again. Little Joe laughed so hard, his cheeks wobbled.

'Again!' he told Tasha.

'No,' Tasha said. 'Eat your porridge.'

'Again!'

'No!'

'Again!'

Jokey-Jokey!

Little Joe banged his spoon hard in the bowl. A great lump of porridge flew out and landed on Tasha's thin cotton cowboy shirt.

'Thank you,' said Tasha. 'Thank you very much.'

Still dripping porridge, she slid off her seat and made for the door.

'*If you're nice to him, he shouldn't give you any trouble at all*,' the voice from the cassette assured her as she slowly climbed the stairs.

Gggrrrr!

Back in the bedroom, Tasha rooted through her cupboard, looking for something else to wear. There wasn't much. Half her clothes were in the mending pile. The other half were in the wash. In the end, just as she feared, Tasha could only find one thing.

Sighing, she pulled it over her head.

It was the pretty red woolly Granny knitted for her.

'Wabbit! Wabbit!'

Nicky stood listening to the list of things he had to get ready for Little Joe.

'*He'll need his big plastic Snoopy lunchbox,*' Mum was saying on the tape. '*And his juice bottle. And his spare pair of underpants. And his dummy. And, of course, Rabbit.*'

Little Joe bounced up and down in his highchair.

'Wabbit!' he shouted. 'Wabbit! Wabbit! Wabbit!'

'Just a minute,' said Nicky. 'I have to find the other things as well. They're just as important as Rabbit.'

Wabbit!

'Wabbit!' Little Joe pounded his fists on the tray in front of him. 'Wabbit! Wabbit! Wabbit!'

Nicky looked round. There, at the end of the table, was the big plastic Snoopy lunchbox.

'Right,' he said. 'That's one. Only four to go.'

He kept looking. The juice bottle was nowhere to be found.

Nor were the spare pair of underpants or the dummy.

'I can't even see Rabbit,' muttered Nicky.

'Wabbit!' screamed Little Joe. 'Wabbit! Wabbit! Wabbit!'

'Just be quiet,' Nicky told Little Joe sternly, unstrapping him and lifting him out of the highchair. 'Just yelling doesn't help. If you want to be useful, go round the house and *look* for things. Don't just stand there yelling Rabbit.'

'Wabbit!' screeched Little Joe. 'Wabbit! Wabbit! Wabbit!'

Nicky shoved his face close to Little Joe's.

'Shut up!' he yelled back. 'Shut up! Shut up!
Shut up!'

'Wabbit!' yelled Little Joe. 'Wabbit! Wabbit!
Wabbit!'

Losing his temper, Nicky snatched a tea
towel off the rack, and hurled it at Little
Joe's head.

Furious, Little Joe snatched the big plastic Snoopy lunchbox off the table, and hurled it at Nicky.

Nicky jumped out of the way, fast.

The lunchbox landed with a crash on the floor. The clasps flew open. Out fell the juice bottle, the spare pair of underpants, the dummy and Rabbit.

'Wabbit!' shrieked Little Joe with glee. 'Wabbit! Wabbit! Wabbit!'

He ran across and scooped Rabbit up in his arms. Then he sat on the floor in the corner and cuddled her, twisting one of her long velvet ears around his finger while Nicky filled the juice bottle, took the sandwich marked 'Joe – Thursday' out of the freezer, and packed him a banana and a nut bar. He was just rinsing the dummy under the tap when Tasha came down again.

'Everything going OK?' she asked him.

'Fine,' Nicky said. 'No problem.'

Their mother's voice came from the tape.

'*Right*,' it was saying. '*Quite sure you've got everything for Joe?*'

'Quite sure, thanks,' Nicky told the tape grimly.

But the voice was checking them over one more time, just to be safe:

'*Big plastic Snoopy lunchbox, juice bottle, spare pair of underpants, dummy and Rabbit?*'

'Wabbit!' said Little Joe ecstatically, wrapping her ear tightly around him and squeezing hard. 'Wabbit! Wabbit! Wabbit!'

I love you, Wabbit.

'Ssssh!'

'*Now,*' said their mother's voice. '*If you're quite sure you've had enough breakfast and you're all packed for school, it's time to reset the alarm clock for one o'clock, and put it next to Daddy's bed* –'

'Without waking him?' demanded Tasha.

'– *without waking him,*' the tape said.

'Serious stuff,' said Tasha, eyeing Little Joe suspiciously.

'We'll need a plan,' agreed Nicky.

First, they tried Plan A. Tasha sat Little Joe
on her knee and sang him nursery rhymes,
very softly, while Nicky fetched the alarm
and reset it, then crept along the landing
towards the big bedroom.

Little Joe tried poking Tasha to make her
sing louder. When it didn't work, he wriggled
out of her lap and rushed off to fetch Nicky.

Tasha rushed after him.

Next, they tried Plan B. Tasha sneaked
away with the alarm clock and Nicky sat
Little Joe on the draining board and told him
the story of the Three Bears while he was

washing up. But Little Joe got excited when
he heard the word 'porridge', and banged his
heels on the cupboard doors.

Nicky lifted him down, and he broke away
and ran after Tasha.

In the end, they used Plan C. Tasha
explained to Little Joe that it was a game,
and he had to be quiet.

'Sssh!' she said, putting a finger on her lips.

'Sssh!' said Little Joe, copying her.

'Quieter than that,' warned Tasha. 'Ssssssh!'

'Ssssssh!' said Little Joe, very, very quietly.

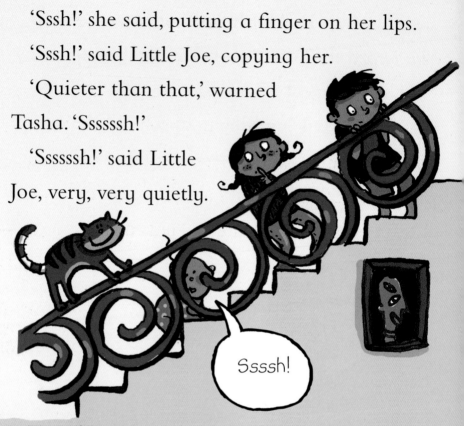

Sssssh!

Together they went up the stairs. Nicky pushed open the door to the big bedroom.

'Ssssssh!' Little Joe said, but he said it quietly.

Daddy lay on his back on his side of the big bed. One arm was flung out, and his head was back. There was nasty black stubble all over his cheeks and his chin, and he was snoring loudly.

'Ssssh!' Little Joe told him sternly. 'Ssssh!'

Nicky crept to the side of the bed and put down the alarm clock, reset for one o'clock. Little Joe followed Nicky, and Tasha followed Joe, in case he suddenly started fussing.

'Sssssh!' Joe warned everyone.

The three of them stood in a line beside the bed and looked down at their stubbly, snoring father. Whenever he reached the main part of each breath, his whole jaw shuddered and a flap of sheet under his nose flew up in the air. There was oil on his forehead and oil under his fingernails, and his pyjamas were not buttoned up.

'Yuk,' Little Joe said. 'Yuk.'

'Too right,' said Tasha. 'If this is what he looks like in the morning, good thing it's Mum who kisses us goodbye.'

Just then their father snored in his sleep, smacking his lips like a chimpanzee, and letting his mouth fall wide open.

'Kiss Daddy goodbye,' Nicky teased Joe.

Joe stuck out his bottom lip.

Hastily, Tasha took his hand and pulled him towards the door.

'Let's just *blow* Daddy a kiss,' she said. 'He'll like that. So will you.'

Joe's lip went in again.

'Smart thinking, Tash,' said Nicky.

The three of them stood in a line by the door, and, one by one, blew a kiss to their sleeping father.

Then they left, shutting the door very quietly behind them.

'Ready?'

As soon as Little Joe had gone off to playgroup with Flora and Mrs Bundy from next door, Nicky and Tasha raced around the house, following orders from the tape.

'*Have you turned off the taps in the bathroom properly? Especially the hot tap?*'

Nicky raced upstairs to check on the hot tap.

'*Is the cat out?*'

Tasha chased the cat out.

'*And don't forget to lock the back door.*'

Tasha locked the back door.

'*Is the oven off?*'

Nicky checked it.

'*And the grill! Don't forget the grill!*'

Nicky checked the grill – twice.

'*Is the fridge door shut?*'

'Yes,' Tasha told the
tape. 'Yes, it's shut.'

'*Have you switched your bedroom light off?*'
Now it was Tasha's turn to race upstairs.

'*And put the cat's dish out on the back
door step?*'

Nicky did that, while Tasha raced
downstairs again.

'*And have you found your jackets and your school bags?*'

Yes!

'Yes, yes, yes.'

'*And taken your lunch money off the shelf?*'

Nicky passed one pile of coins to Tasha, and dropped the others in his pocket.

'Yes, yes, yes.'

'*What else?*' the voice on the tape said, stopping for a think.

'Have you fed the elephant?'
muttered Tasha.

'And switched on the rocketship parked on
the roof?' added Nicky.

'And locked Mad Old Aunt Lucy in the
coal cellar?'

'With her rat poison sandwiches?'

'*I can't think of anything else,*' said the voice on the tape. '*I hope there's nothing I've forgotten.*'

'Nicky's sub-machine gun?' suggested Tasha.

'Tasha's dirt-bike?'

VVVR°°°°M

'Nicky's pet armadillo?'
'Tasha's diamonds?'

'*Of course!*' the tape said. '*Your homework reading books! They're stuck in the toast rack.*'

Nicky rushed over to fetch them.

'*That's it, then,*' said the tape. '*I think you're probably ready to go. Now, without waking Daddy, put on your jackets, pick up your school bags and tiptoe to the front door. Drop the catch on the lock, and pull the door closed behind you.*'

'Very quietly,' prompted Tasha.

'*Very quietly,*' said the tape.

Together, they pulled on their jackets
and picked up their school bags. They didn't
wait for the voice on the tape. They started
chanting the next bit all by themselves.

'*And be good, and be careful, and stick together
till you get to the main road, and make sure you
cross with the lollipop lady.*'

Nicky and Tasha had finished chanting the daily speech well before the voice on the tape limped to the end.

Then they tiptoed away from the cassette-player towards the front door.

'*Goodbye, darlings,*' the voice on the tape called after them.

'Goodbye,' called Nicky and Tasha.

They let the catch down, and pulled the door shut and locked it behind them. Then they turned to one another, and said, 'Phew!'

Back in the kitchen, there was a silence as the tape ran on towards its end. Then, suddenly, the voice said, '*Phew!*'

And it fell silent.